# LI'L LYNN
## Tells It Herself

A Novella-zation of the Graphic Novel
*Li'l Lynn: **The Joy of Childhood and Other Myths***

Also by Charles Shearer

*Li'l Lynn Tells It Herself: A Novella-zation*

## https://charlesshearer.info

ISBN 978-0-9984798-0-4
Novella, Young Adult Fiction.

FIRST EDITION, 2017     REVISION, 2022

Production: 2016 December and 2017 June in Amherst, NY, USA.
"Scenario: Coffee Shop": 2015 December in Decatur, GA, USA.
Exclusive Bonus Comic: 2017 June 30 and July 1 in Amherst, NY, USA.

# TABLE OF CONTENTS

# A Preface by the Author

This prose-and-pictures canonical complement to the original graphic novel *Li'l Lynn: The Joy of Childhood and Other Myths* serves as a genuine first-hand account and a biased second opinion, as little Lynn Herr tells the story herself.

Intended to be in complete accord with the original graphic novel, while also deliberately differing from it in notable regards, this illustrated novella features many hitherto unknown happenings in this formative phase of young Lynn's life, shares the heart and mind of our eponymous protagonist with us as only her own words can, and is adorned with styles and media of artwork that, all in all, set it apart as a fully-fledged work in its own right.

Charles Shearer
Amherst, NY
2017 June 16

*An excerpt from the original graphic novel*

# 1:

# Springtime

Aunt Celly is good at making things. She says it's cheaper to buy ingredients and then turn them into real things, because if you buy stuff already finished by other people, it costs more money, so those people can get paid. And if you buy things most people don't want right now, it's also cheaper. So it's too hot to wear the vest Aunt Celly improved for me. She bought it really cheap, and then sewed things onto it, to make me like it more. It'll be really nice, later.

Restaurants cost a lot, too, and I'm not allowed in Just Aunt Celly Kind Of Places, so we mostly stay at home after I get back from school. Aunt Celly and Colossus were already here all day, though. Aunt Celly has to stay, because her job is with folders and stacks of paper sent in the mail. They're books, but not the finished kind with covers and drawings. She changes the language of the words, and then sends them back and gets paid, and then the books show up in stores whenever the publisher feels like it. That means after a long time. I think it would cost less if the customers in the stores could just buy the old versions, but they can't understand the real words. That's how Aunt Celly gets money for being really smart. Not just anyone can do that job.

Colossus also sort of has a job. He protects the house and keeps an eye on things. It's like how a lion just spends every day doing nothing but eating what the lionesses bring him. Until that one day when he springs into action and saves them from bad guys! So Colossus is really looking out for us. Even if it doesn't look like it, all the time.

*Facing page:*
**"My Family"**

*Lynn Herr*
*Pencil on paper*
*Aunt Celly's door*

*Lynn's comment:*
*All three of us. My family is pretty good.*

~~~

So it's getting late. I always forget to notice, so Aunt Celly tells me. Colossus doesn't ever care what time it is, except when I'm already asleep. That's when he wakes up from his pillow in the living room and then he goes to sleep on his real bed in my room. He's really strict about it. I don't hear him come in, but I do hear his snorting when he's asleep, because it sometimes wakes me up. But it's not time for that, yet. I was talking about it just starting to get late.

Aunt Celly always gives me juice in just a little cup, because it's getting late, as I already said. It's pretty good. Her drink smells like a gas station. The outside part, where all the cars are. I can't figure out why she likes it. Tonight, she's telling me a story about her youth. She's only twenty-seven, though, which I don't think is very old. My teacher at school has kids who are older than her. College just seems like a long time ago, to Aunt Celly. She calls it "like someone else's life." I think she's sad. Sometimes I'm a little sad, too, but then I think about Aunt Celly and Colossus, and I feel better.

Oh, tonight's story is about the time in college when Aunt Celly stayed up all night, playing with friends, and the next day, she was seeing things that weren't there. What a weird story! I think the moral is about how people have to get enough sleep, or else their brains go haywire. That sounds worse than just being regular-tired. My bed is my favorite place, though, so I don't mind being tired. Waiting to go to sleep is when I think about things that happened during the day.

Actually, I don't understand some other things Aunt Celly tells me, but I always listen to her. I like to share the stories with my teacher. One day, I came home, and Aunt Celly said she got a phone-call from the school. I thought I was in trouble, but Aunt Celly was laughing about the whole thing. She started telling me even weirder stories, after that. But when she tucks me in, she just talks to me quietly about what we're doing tomorrow. It's my favorite time, in my favorite place. I'm really glad I have such a great aunt. Tomorrow is the weekend, so we'll do our weekend stuff.

~ ~ ~

I heard Colossus used to be athletic. He's more of a scholar and a gentleman now, but he still needs some exercise. The park is nice for that, and all of it's outside, so Aunt Celly comes along to adult-supervise me. Her favorite bench is far away enough that I can't smell her smoking.

I don't like remembering this, but I once called her "Aunt Smelly" (because of the smoking) and she heard me say it. I thought it was a good joke, because the words rhyme, but I was really sorry. She didn't say she was upset, but I could tell she was, because she called me just by my regular first name, like she wasn't my Aunt Celly. I got the message. That was a long time ago, and I don't tell

Colossus those kinds of jokes anymore, so everything's okay again. He mostly likes word games, especially the one where I say a word and then I say another word that starts with the same letter as the end of the first word, and he likes hearing about what I've been learning at school. I try to remember the lessons, so I can teach them to him. He's a good listener, and very thoughtful. We don't end up getting much exercise, though, because Colossus gets tired easily, and I don't want to give him a hard time.

*Facing page:*
**"Exact Portrait of Colossus"**

*Lynn Herr*
*Pencil on paper*
*Living room wall*

*Lynn's comment:*
*I was able to make this one so accurate,*
*because Colossus was holding still while I*
*was drawing him.*

He's not getting any younger. His wrinkles make him look really old, but Aunt Celly says he always looked like that. She remembers when he was a puppy, but I don't, because I wasn't born yet. Colossus was the runt of the litter, which Aunt Celly once told me is "redundant." I've seen pictures of them both, from a long time ago. Colossus is a lot younger than Aunt Celly, but also a lot older, because Dog Time is different. So a day for me is like a week for Colossus. It's no wonder he misses me so much when I'm at school, but I miss him, too, so it's alright.

That makes sense, but Aunt Celly also told me Adult Time is even more different. That's why to her, every day feels like it will never end but a month goes by before she knows it. I can't explain it any better than that. It's really weird that Aunt Celly and Colossus spend all day together in the same house, but time feels so different to them. I don't know why it can't just be regular. Colossus doesn't know, either. That's the sort of thing I talk with him about.

It was a pretty good day. I thought of a lot of words for my game. Colossus explored around the park for a little while. There was a loud girl who tried to play with him, but he wasn't really into it.

Aunt Celly took me to the restaurant where they let Colossus come in, because he's well behaved, and we sometimes get a discount because Aunt Celly once wrote signs and menus for them in another language. The manager who knows her was there, so we got the discount. That was lucky. Aunt Celly told me we shouldn't abuse it, though, because we do have our pride. So we only go there once per week. Does that feel like all the time, though, to Aunt Celly?

My subscription came in, while we were out! Aunt Celly suddenly looked tired, so we'll wait until tomorrow, to read it. She said it'll be a long day. That's what she says about most days. I'm glad we'll have so much time for it and not be in a hurry. Aunt Celly forgot to talk about it while she was tucking me in, so I reminded her. I can't wait to go to sleep and wake up! Aunt Celly said she was terribly excited, too.

~~~

After I ate breakfast, I spent a while trying to find the new issue of my subscription. It wasn't on the couch, where I remember leaving it, yesterday. I put it there, instead of with my Collection, so we'd remember it right away. My Collection is impressive, and I take good care of it. It's on the middle shelf in my room, instead of on the bottom one, so Colossus won't mess it up on accident. He would feel just awful about it, if he ever did. And Aunt Celly promised she'll never go anywhere near it for as long as she lives.

Oh, finally! I found the new issue under some papers on the table.

I can read the issues by myself alright, but I like it better when Aunt Celly reads them with me. I can see the pictures just fine, but she still tells me what's happening in them, anyway, and she points out a lot of things I don't notice. She doesn't like Peppy Young Lab Assistant Kittyson. Of course, no one is supposed to like him, because he's so dumb, and he keeps ruining scientific progress.

*Facing page:*
**"Kittyson Ruining Scientific Progress"**

*Lynn Herr*
*Chalk on sidewalk*
*Had been in front of the house*

*Lynn's comment:*
*Kittyson caused an explosion and dropped important test tubes with chemicals in them. Lab Master is trying to stop him, but it's too late. It's always too late.*

Aunt Celly just calls Kittyson "the cat wearing a tie." She refuses to say his actual name. I guess she thinks Lab Master is alright, though, because she just calls him "Lab Master" and doesn't make fun of him. I think it's because he's a gentleman. He also wears a tie, and it looks nice on him. Ties are actually really hard to tie. Aunt Celly knows how to do it without even putting it on! She learned it from a clothing store job she used to have. So I'll get to be Lab Master for Hallowe'en. Yes, it's supposed to have an apostrophe in it. I really hate it when people tell me it's wrong. Aunt Celly once saw it spelled like that in an old book in a library. Also, her job is with words, anyway, so she knows what she's talking about.

Lab Master is really good. I respect him. He does research and other things for his university. I think he invents new chemicals. Medicine, maybe?

*Next three pages:*
***"Lab Master & Kittyson: Special Issue"***

*Lynn Herr*
*Pencil on paper, both sides*
*The Collection*

*Lynn's comment:*
*This isn't a real issue. Aunt Celly says it does look just about as good as one, though.*

He also teaches science classes. His name is a joke about the kind of dog he is. He's a "black lab." I don't know what kind of cat Kittyson is, though. Aunt Celly says it doesn't matter, with cats. We're both Dog People, but my Grandpa Herr is a Cat Person. One of his cats just hides all the time, so it's hard to see it up close. The other one was just staring out the window, the whole time when we visited. Aunt Celly said having a fishtank is even worse, because at least a cat is easy to move out of the way. Fish are not pets. Aunt Celly had fish and cats when she was a kid, and she didn't like them very much, I think. Dogs are great, though. They're territorial and loyal and friendly. That's why Colossus protects us so well and things are pretty good at home.

Anyway, Aunt Celly's voices for the word balloons are funny. Kittyson only talks in grunts. I don't know how Aunt Celly makes such a deep voice for him. It's hard for me to do for very long. Lab Master sounds like he thinks Kittyson is a kindergartener, instead of a graduate student, which he's actually supposed to be. Aunt Celly used to know a lot of real graduate students, though, and maybe that's how they really are. By the way, that means people who finished school but still won't leave and get a job.

In this issue, Lab Master is in a top-secret new laboratory no one else is supposed to know about, and he's almost finished a really good and difficult experiment. But then Kittyson shows up, and Lab Master is really surprised or mad about it and wants to know how Kittyson found out about the lab and got through the Anti-Kittyson Security

System. Anyway, Kittyson wants to help with finishing the experiment, because he's supposed to be a Peppy Young Lab Assistant, but then he just messes everything up at the last possible moment and Lab Master gets upset.

It's really neat that Aunt Celly guessed most of the story before much of anything happened yet. I think she really could give up on her career and just write for "Lab Master and Kittyson" instead of ever working again, but she wouldn't want her real name printed in the issues.

~ ~ ~

So we're doing our Every Evening Little Drinks, and Aunt Celly is telling me about her first ex-boyfriend. She started talking about this, because I said when I get married, I hope it'll be with a scientist. Aunt Celly didn't get married with the ex-boyfriend, and he wasn't a scientist, but this made her think about him, anyway. Teenagers think really good things and really bad things will last forever, but actually, teenagers know even less than little kids do. So Aunt Celly's first relationship was a real eye-opener. That means it made her stop being an idiot. She doesn't have a picture of the first ex-boyfriend. Not anymore.

But she has a lot of other pictures. She keeps them in a shoebox in her room, instead of in picture frames, except for one picture of her and my dad from when they were teenagers at a music camp. I don't know what happened to that accordion, but I have his smaller one in my room. It used to be his back-up. I can play it just a little bit. Aunt

Celly still has that same violin that's in the picture, but I've never heard her play it. That picture of them is on her desk, where she does her job.

Anyway, Aunt Celly had liked her first ex-boyfriend, before they broke up, mostly because he had a car, so he could take her to nice places. It's weird that some teenagers have cars, but some adults don't. Aunt Celly wasn't an aunt yet, in the story, because I wasn't born yet. And even before that, Not Yet Aunt Celly was once my age! That's also weird, but it makes sense, because people have to be kids before they can be adults. That's why I was talking about getting married, someday, when I'm a grown-up. Also, getting married is popular in a lot of movies I've seen. It's the reward at the end, for doing a good job and letting the bad guy kill himself on accident. So it must be great!

As I said, Aunt Celly's story tonight doesn't end like that. It's still fun, though. It's about the first ex-boyfriend driving her to a lake, and they had a party with some other people she didn't know. The end of the story is about how she didn't come back home until the next day, and got in huge trouble with Grandpa Herr. He wasn't a grandfather yet, but he was afraid Not Yet Aunt Celly might make him one, any day now, so if she wanted to keep living under his roof and having food to eat, she had to kick the boyfriend to the curb. Those were the exact words. Aunt Celly says I should tell the story to my teacher.

~~~

I'm not sure if that was a good idea or not. I thought I might be in trouble, but my teacher said no, I'm not the one to blame for this. He's really nice. He gave me a letter to take home and get signed. Yes, I know the drill, by now. I always put the letters in my lunchbox right away, so I won't leave them at school, on accident.

The loud girl from the park really does go to my school. She's just in a different homeroom, so I didn't see her, before. I hope she won't want to keep sitting with me at Lunch Time. She actually thinks Kittyson is a good character! Better than Lab Master!? We can never be friends.

Art Time is my favorite. That's when the Art Lady comes to our room, and our regular teacher just sort of walks around and keeps an eye on things. We're cutting up pieces of color-paper and making pictures with them. No pencils or markers are allowed in this activity.

*Next page:*
**"Colossus"**

*Lynn Herr*
*Color-paper and glue*
*Classroom bulletin board*

*Lynn's comment:*
*This won a prize!*

The last time we did this, I made a picture of Colossus. I even made all of his important wrinkles. But the other kids thought he was a bulldog. I absolutely hate it when people do that!

This time, I'm making a picture of Aunt Celly. She already has a lot of different pictures I made of her, but this is going to be the best one. She's kind of hard to draw, so this way is easier. Her cigarettes are black, so I had to cut out little pieces of black paper, instead of just drawing lines with a marker or something. She puts out her cigarettes by squeezing near the burning part until it falls on the sidewalk, and then she throws the mouth part of it in the trash. She learned it from an army guy. I can explain it alright, but it's really hard to show with paper. Now my teacher is taking back the letter, to add something to it.

It rained for just a minute. The other kids in my class were looking out the window, like they never saw rain, before. That's like what happens when a dog comes up to the fence during Free Play Time.

~~~

Aunt Celly swears I'm not in trouble, but she keeps acting weird about the letter. They don't usually bother her, like this. I think showing her my new artwork will make her feel better. I had to take it home with me, anyway.

It didn't really work.

But anyway, while we were having our Little Drinks, Aunt Celly told me about how smoking can be bad for people's health, but it can also help people's moods, which is good for their health. Some other adult things are like that, also. I guess that makes sense. It's about doing those kinds of things just a little bit or only sometimes, not all the time or too much. But some other kinds of things are always really bad, so I should never do them at all. She looks serious about it. I always believe her, of course, but this time, especially. I just wonder what the things I'm never supposed to do are. Aunt Celly will tell me about them when I'm older, so I don't have to sweat about it yet.

*Facing page:*
**"Aunt Celly"**

*Lynn Herr*
*Color-paper and glue*
*Not on the classrooom bulletin board*

*Lynn's comment:*
*My teacher wouldn't put this up, even though*
*I worked hard on it.*

~~~

I always do the maze on the back of my "Lab Master and Kittyson" cereal box with just my eyes, so I won't mess up the box. Before we throw it away, when it's empty, Aunt Celly always cuts out the back for me and lets me save it in my Collection. So it's not just my subscription issues. Those things are the Frivolous Luxuries I'm Allowed To Have. Aunt Celly's usual kind of breakfast costs a lot less money than mine. I know, because she tells me. Her cereal is just oats she soaks in milk for a few minutes. It doesn't really taste like anything. She also makes toast and coffee, and feeds Colossus, and then makes my lunch. It's cheaper than buying the school lunch every day. So Aunt Celly is busy on most mornings. To be honest, I feel kind of busy then, too, because I double-check my homework for mistakes. One time, I missed one the night before and also the next morning, and I was really sad about getting a red mark. I normally never cry at school.

I was thinking about how people have to make money, so they can get other people to do things for them. A long time ago, there wasn't any money, because it wasn't discovered yet. People probably had to do everything by themselves, so they had to cook their own food in restaurants, for example. Life Skills Time made me think about this. In the class, there was just one Class Dollar for each student, at first. Someone could buy one thing, so they lose the Dollar, and then they do one job and end up with one Dollar again. Pretty simple. But then the teacher gave everybody more Dollars. He called it "putting more money into the economy." So a piece of money wasn't worth as much as it used to be, because there were a lot more of them, so everything cost a bigger number of Dollars, but it was still the same thing it used to be. I was trying to save my Dollars, but I was still supposed to spend some of them, or else I would starve, since I was one of the Engineers instead of one of the Farmers. We didn't get to pick our jobs. There wasn't one for "scientist," anyway. It was a really neat game. I like how there wasn't a prize for whoever had the most money at the end, since it wasn't me.

The bus ride home takes a while, so I'm trying to tell the loud girl from the park and from Lunch Time about what I think people did before there was money, and also about the game my homeroom played, but I can't get her to understand what I mean. Anyway, her name is Ashley Weir. Our stops are close-by. I never noticed until recently.

~~~

When Aunt Celly was in college, she had a lot of friends. Most of them were guys, instead of other women. I thought this was strange, but then Aunt Celly explained about how although little boys are mean to girls they like, gentlemen are careful and polite to all ladies. That's a difference between a mere boy and a real man. So her guy-friends in college treated her nicely, and tried not to say bad words around her. That was different from high school, but Aunt Celly in high school didn't know that, yet. I'm supposed to remember this, so I'll never tolerate disrespect. Aunt Celly was telling me a Pearl of Wisdom like this, and it wasn't even time for Little Drinks, yet! We were still just having dinner. So that one was a bonus.

She puts a lot of little extra things into the dinners she makes, so they taste interesting, like they came from a restaurant we can't afford to go to. It's the one pretty good meal she has to allow herself, every day, so she won't go crazy. I'm always full after dinner, and I like to keep tasting it for a while after I'm done eating. That's why I don't drink anything, at the end. I also like the leftovers, because they seem a little different after a day or so, and sometimes we have leftovers from two previous different days, so it's especially like a completely new dinner. Aunt Celly appreciates my approval. She invented cooking like this, when she started taking care of me. It was before I can actually remember. It feels like a long time for both of us. When she says "a hundred years," it's not for real, of course. She says that about some other things, too. It's her favorite joke.

Anyway, she still has friends, but now they're mostly "old friends." That means she doesn't get to visit them, anymore, and they only sometimes talk with her on the phone or write letters. I once talked to Aunt Celly over the phone, but it felt like she wasn't real and I was just talking to her voice, because I couldn't see her. So I couldn't think of much to say. But when Aunt Celly is quiet during a phone call, it's only because she's listening to what an old friend is saying. They take turns like that. Now she's taking the phone into her room, for privacy. I understand. But she'll probably want to tell me the juicy details, later. I'll probably never meet any of her old friends, anyway, so it's okay if I know their business.

It turns out the old friend on the phone just got married with another old friend of theirs. The wedding was a secret to everyone, until it already happened. It's called "eloping." I had never heard of that kind of wedding. Aunt Celly already knew what it was, but she was surprised her old friends would do something like that. She had a whole lot to say while she was on the phone, but she didn't feel like talking very much about it with me, afterward. I didn't expect that. She was thinking a lot, instead. Maybe she still wanted privacy by herself. She looked at me, and I thought she was actually scared of something for a second, but then she looked normal again. She told me she's sorry for blanking out like that. Then she gave me my normal Little Drink of juice, but she didn't make anything for herself. I felt weird about that, so I give her the bottom half of my juice, and after a little while, she tucked me in. She promised to tell me what's going on with her, after she figures it all out, herself. Everything will be okay again.

~~~

I was waiting all day to hear about what's on Aunt Celly's mind. Finally, she told me she feels weird about how she used to be so close to her friends, but by now, she's so out of the loop, they almost feel like strangers to her. And when people get married, they especially stop hanging out with their single friends, anyway. That's why Aunt Celly says weddings and funerals are kind of the same thing. They both make people say goodbye to friends or relatives who used to have lives.

We talk about death, sometimes. It's no stranger to our family. This topic really bothers Aunt Celly. I don't want her to be sad.

~~~

This is the longest bus ride of my life. Why does Ashley keep telling me her birthday is next week?

*Facing page:*
**"How Ashley Tells Me Everything"**

*Lynn Herr*
*Pencil on paper*
*Inside a folder*

*Lynn's comment:*
*Ashley is loud and I don't like her.*

She doesn't like how it'll be on a school day. Well, what am I supposed to do about it!? I just know she's going to keep talking about this, at Lunch Time. I can't get her to leave me alone.

Music Time is pretty good. It's only once a week, though. There's an accordion in the back room, but it's too big and heavy for me to use, and the piano is so important, only the music teacher gets to use it. We get things like xylophones, instead. There are a whole bunch of them in the back room, because they're a lot cheaper than real instruments. The music classroom has posters of lots of different kinds of instruments from all over the world. They're all different, but also kind of the same. Aunt Celly once said they're like different languages for saying similar ideas. She would know that sort of thing. She also told me drums don't really count, though, since they can't play songs. Drummers are sensitive about it. So I shouldn't bring it up with them, if I ever meet any.

It bothers me when people say "note" instead of "tone." Notes are written on paper, and tones are the actual sounds. That's what the words mean! Even the music teacher gets this wrong, all the time. That's another thing I'm not supposed to bring up.

At home, I mostly just like playing scales and arpeggios, and I can even do multiple octaves, sometimes! That's an advanced technique. But in Music Time, we don't learn that sort of thing, or about key signatures, either. We only do melodies. Those are like scales, but with the tones played out of order and in certain times that have to be exactly right, or else everyone can tell I'm doing it wrong. It's really stressful. Good thing that's just the end part of Music Time. The rest of it is called "free warm-up." That's when we can do whatever we want, and my regular teacher ditches us in a hurry.

If I barely get to eat my lunch at all, should it still be called Lunch Time? My birthday is always during summer vacation, so it will never be on a school day. Aunt Celly and I get all day to celebrate it. So maybe I can kind of understand what's bothering Ashley, but then she said scales and arpeggios are boring! This is why I don't like talking to her. I hope tomorrow will be different.

~~~

It's not.

I think I'm being punished for something. Whatever it is, I'm very sorry! Ashley's still talking about her birthday. Now she says her mom will celebrate it with her early, this weekend, so it won't be on a school day. Still not sure why I have to hear about it, though. And now is only the bus ride to school. There's still Lunch Time and the ride back home. Today is going to take a hundred years.

My class is watching a nature documentary. I didn't think kangaroos were real, but I guess they are. They're better at hopping than walking, like rabbits. After the tape was done, we talked about how humans and animals can share the Earth. A lot of people eat animals, but not many animals eat people. There used to be more that did, but they went extinct and I think people started living in houses and cities instead of in the woods. Some animals moved in with people and became pets. I heard dogs like Colossus can't survive in the wilderness, because nature would never produce such a creature, in the first place. But I would never tell him that.

For crying out loud, may I please just eat my lunch!? Honestly, I don't care about Ashley's birthday party, tomorrow. What's it got to do with me? And what's with all the questions about Colossus?

I told Aunt Celly my joke about today taking a hundred years. She thought it was funny. Wow, I almost never make her laugh! Anyway, she's getting back to normal. I'm really glad. It's like how I said everything will be okay again, and now it is. We don't have any special plans for tomorrow, so we'll just get to take it easy.

~~~

For real!? How did Ashley find my house!? And who said she could bother me on the weekend, I'd like to know!

I woke up Aunt Celly. I don't actually have to go to Ashley's birthday party, do I? Yes, I know her from school. No, I don't have to bring her a present. Yes, I can walk to her house. It looks close-by, on the map she drew for me. Colossus was also invited. He's taking it better than I am. But do we have to be allowed to go? Aunt Celly says I have to bite the bullet and be a big girl and handle my business.

It's that sort of thing. Ashley's waiting for me and Colossus at her house, so we have to get a move on.

I'm used to following maps. On my last birthday, Aunt Celly found an ancient treasure map that came out of nowhere, and she said I should maybe follow it and see where it goes. I did, and it took me to a key I never saw before. I had to figure out where the key went, so I looked around for things with locks on them. It didn't work on Aunt Celly's footlocker. I still don't know what's in there. The key actually went to a little box that looked like a treasure chest. There was a riddle inside. It was kind of tricky, so Aunt Celly helped me figure it out. The answer was "refrigerator." We had to think of a place where it's always light when you look inside, but always dark when you don't. So we went to the fridge and opened it, and there was a present for me, from Aunt Celly! It wasn't even food, though, so I never would've thought of looking there. It turned out Aunt Celly drew the map, herself, and then she made it look old by burning the edges with a lighter. That's pretty clever. And she set up the rest of the adventure, too. Aunt Celly's way of giving me presents is better than just spending a lot of money and being boring about it. Also, most people don't do this like we do, because they're not as cool as Aunt Celly. I still have the treasure map, in my room. But I forgot what the actual present was.

Ashley's map is different, though. It's just on a regular piece of paper. I guess she didn't know about the advanced techniques.

Wow! Ashley's house is really nice on the inside.

There are pictures in frames on the walls, and shelves full of things, and pillows on the floor. There's so much stuff. Am I allowed to touch any of it? Ashley's mom is friendly. She smiles a lot. I call her "Mrs Weir," when I talk to her. I thought birthday parties are supposed to have lots of guests, but it looks like it's just going to be me and Colossus, at this one. I hope we do all the party stuff right, and not embarrass ourselves.

Wow, again! Now I know why we didn't have to bring Ashley a present. She already has so many of them, in a big pile on the floor. They're wrapped up, which is nice, but that's not the same as going on a treasure hunt.

*Facing page:*
**"Ashley's Birthday Presents"**

*Lynn Herr*
*Pencil on paper*
*Somewhere or other*

*Lynn's comment:*
*She didn't really use a ladder. That part is a joke. A ladder wouldn't actually fit inside the house.*

Some of Ashley's presents are those life-size Lab Master and Kittyson stuffed-animals I always see in the back of my subscription issues, next to the fan letters. Mrs Weir's voices for Lab Master and Kittyson are so different from what I'm used to! She makes Kittyson talk really fast and excited, and the "s" sounds come out like "th," instead. It's pretty funny, but I still don't like Kittyson. Mrs Weir's version of Lab Master sounds really manly and smart, like he's thinking carefully about everything he says. That's so like him! And he's really handsome, in person.

I wish Lab Master was my teacher, or my boss at work. I would be a really good lab assistant. Much better than Kittyson! I could help Lab Master make scientific breakthroughs, and the university would give him an award, and he would dedicate it to me in his acceptance speech at the party.

*Next three pages:*
***"Lab Master & Lynn #1"***

*Lynn Herr*
*Pencil on paper*
*The Collection*

*Lynn's comment:*
*No more Kittyson at all!*

Kittyson wouldn't be invited, of course, but he would show up, anyway, because that sort of thing is what happens in the real stories.

Mrs Weir asks me a lot of questions about my family. She already knows Colossus, because I had to bring him with me, but she doesn't know Aunt Celly. So I explain about how Aunt Celly's real name is "Celesta Herr." Her real first name is also the name of a musical instrument no one's heard of anymore. It's not even on any of the posters in the music classroom, so the other kids didn't believe me. But I don't think anyone's actually called Aunt Celly out loud by her real name, in a long time. She only uses it for business purposes, like with her job, and that's only through writing. Our last name is from one of The Old Countries. I really, really hate it when people say it wrong, like when they read it from somewhere for the first time. Once, the principal said it wrong over the intercom, and everyone in my class laughed. I just wanted to disappear from the planet.

Mrs Weir's first name is "Sandra," but her friends call her "Sandy." The "a" sounds different in each one. That sort of thing is important to get right.

Talking about this sort of thing reminded me about how some people use their middle name instead of their first name, and they have to spend their whole life explaining it to everyone. Middle names aren't really supposed to be used for anything. Except when a family names two people exactly the same, for some reason. How dumb. But they still have to be called something different, or else no one will know who they're talking about. And some people actually have two middle names! Kittyson's real name is James Matthew Francis Kittyson the Third. It's even got a number in it. That's the worst thing I ever heard of. Anyway, I guess my whole point is about how no one ever calls me "Eliseba," and I hope they never do.

Mrs Weir is a "physical therapist," so her job is to help people's bodies work better and not hurt anymore. That sounds great! Also, I think she makes a lot of money at it. She spends all day with other people, like I do at school. I think most jobs are like that, but Aunt Celly's isn't. She has to be by herself when she's doing her work, or else she'll be distracted and not get anything done and we'll starve. That must be lonely. Oh, it would be great if Aunt Celly and Mrs Weir got to be friends! Mrs Weir thinks that's a good idea, too. They could call each other "Celly" and "Sandy," and our houses are really close-by, so they could visit a lot. But then Ashley would probably come along, too, so I'll have to think about it some more.

Now we're having the pizza and other stuff Mrs Weir got delivered for lunch, and it's strange how we don't all sit around the same place. At my house, I always eat at the table with Aunt Celly, and Colossus watches us from the floor, to see what we'll give him. He's a little confused right now, here at Ashley's house, because everyone's in a different place. But he's not allowed to have pizza, anyway, because it might have onions in it. We don't keep chocolate at home, either, just to be safe. Also, Aunt Celly and chocolate have an abusive relationship (that's what she calls it), so she would spend all day eating chocolate by herself while I'm at school, if she could get away with it. It's also called a "slippery slope." We sometimes just eat dinners right out of the pan or whatever, but Mrs Weir and Ashley are using their own separate plates and everything else. Also, they use forks to eat pizza, for some reason, so they must have a lot of dishes to wash, all the time. Or maybe they're just doing like this today, because it's a special occasion.

The really strange thing is they eat the real part of the pizza first, and then maybe they eat the crust. Or maybe not. It makes more sense to eat the crust first, because it's the just-okay part, and then to eat the real part where the cheese and toppings are. It saves the best for last. What's really good is to eat two crusts first, so then I would get two real parts in a row! No one really wants to eat the crust after they already ate the real part, so sometimes they just throw the crust away, even though they knew it would be a part of the pizza but they paid money for it, anyway. Aunt Celly practically has a fit, whenever she sees someone wasting food like that. I don't blame her. But I'll do like Ashley and her mom are doing, just for today.

Oh, there was no birthday cake! That's because Ashley doesn't do well with lots of sugar. It makes her bounce off the walls, and then she crashes. That's how Mrs Weir explained it. Instead, we watched a movie, and I swear, Ashley was talking through the whole thing! Why would anyone do that!? It was a movie I never saw before, so I missed some parts of it and I don't know everything that happened. The parts Ashley did let me hear were pretty good. Then, the second movie we watched was one I saw before. Ashley kept yelling things like "Look at this part!" even though I was already looking, of course, and I knew what was going to happen. Mrs Weir was doing some other things. Reading a book, I guess, but I'm not sure, because I was trying to watch the movies. In one of them, there was a dog barking, and Colossus woke up and barked back at it. Ashley acted like it was a magic trick. Actually, I was also a little surprised, since Colossus is normally quiet. Except for his snorting while he's asleep. And his panting when he's tired. And any time when he's eating.

Now that I think about it, he does tend to be noisy. So never mind what I said.

*Next page:*
**"Colossus Begging"**

*Lynn Herr*
*Pencil on paper*
*Living room wall*

*Lynn's comment:*
*He just stares at us. We understand what he means.*

It takes a long time to watch two movies, so I was getting a little hungry again. Mrs Weir made sandwiches for us. We ate them on the couch, and used plates. Different ones from earlier. We didn't have to use forks with the sandwiches, though, because that would be going too far. Maybe Ashley and her mom don't really use their dinner table for much. We found something safe for Colossus to eat, too. (He was kind of noisy.) Mrs Weir read the ingredients for us. I know everything dogs shouldn't eat.

~~~

I had a lot of fun at the party. Poor Colossus, though, he's really tired from all the excitement and attention. Ashley really likes him, but she doesn't understand he's retired from sports, in his Golden Years. I know how to be patient with him while he's resting, so we'll get home whenever we get there. There's no hurry. It's already starting to get late, though, and I barely even got to see Aunt Celly today. That almost never happens. I did call her at home, after the first movie, because Mrs Weir said I should. But that doesn't count, because it was over the phone. There are so many things I want to ask Aunt Celly about.

I was so happy to see her and to tell her all about the party, that I forgot most of the questions. She got a lot of work done by herself while Colossus and I were gone, so she had a good day, too. We had a small dinner and did Little Drinks at the same time, because of how late it was. Just this once. Colossus usually waits under the table during dinner, then he takes a nap in the living room during Little Drinks. But tonight wasn't usual, so he wasn't sure what to do. It reminded me of one of my questions. Aunt Celly's answer was about how Eating Together At The Table happens in some families but not in all of them. In ours, it skips generations. So my grandparents weren't big on it, but Aunt Celly is, because Family Togetherness actually means something to her.

My bed is so comfortable. I'm thinking about as many things as I can, before I fall asleep. Ashley seems kind of alright as a friend, after all. I like Mrs Weir better, though. Ashley's lucky to have such a nice mom.

~~~

Oh, what a weird dream! It was kind of scary, so I guess maybe it was a nightmare. Not a very bad one, though. Anyway, I feel better now, because I can hear Colossus snorting. That means he's asleep in his real bed, next to mine. It's too dark to see him very well, but I can tell he's doing fine. I'll leave the light off, and not bother him. I think I wasn't asleep for very long, because Aunt Celly is still awake, at the dinner table. She's having a Little Drink by herself. It's okay for her to stay up late tonight, because tomorrow is still the weekend.

Aunt Celly's carrying me back to bed. I'm still little enough that she can just barely do that, so she always calls me "Little Lynn." It's easier to say it like "Li'l Lynn," though, so that's what she does. And she says the "Lynn" louder than the "Li'l." Once I grow up enough and get too big for this, she'll have to call me something else, and she does already have something in mind, but I'll always call her "Aunt Celly," no matter what.

Since we're talking about things, I remembered another one of the questions I had about today, from the party. Aunt Celly's answer is about how when she was younger, her family made everyone say "I love you" to each other, all the time, even though no one was actually very close. So it felt like it didn't really mean much of anything. Or it really just meant "goodbye" or "good night" or "thank you." The whole thing felt phony, to her, and it bothered her more and more, to have to keep saying it, every day, just to avoid causing a scene. But now, Aunt Celly is an adult, living under her own roof. So she doesn't have to say it all the time anymore, and neither do I. She never wants me to feel forced into it, like she used to be. That's the reason.

*Facing page:*
**"Colossus"**

*Ashley Weir*
*Color-paper and glue*
*Under a stack of papers*

*Lynn's comment:*
*Ashley gave me this. Ugh. I hate it.*
*Colossus doesn't look anything like that.*

# 2:

# Summer

Aunt Celly's right. It is really nice how Ashley and I get such a long vacation from society's demands. We're supposed to enjoy this while it lasts. School was sometimes fun, though, so I didn't mind going there. Aunt Celly and Mrs Weir have to keep working at their jobs, pretty much every week.

Mrs Weir's clinic is okay for hanging out. It's near some other buildings, like offices for dentists and some other kinds of doctors, and the different buildings have outside hallways between them. They even have coverings, in case it rains. There's a lot of pavement, so Ashley and I have lots of space for drawing with chalk. She said she wants to "bomb" the parking lot. That means covering it with drawings. Not blowing it up. But her mom said we can only "bomb" the sidewalks, not the parking spaces or driveways, or else drivers might run us over, on accident. I think that's what Ashley really meant, anyway. The spots where not many people walk get filled up, so then we have to start drawing where most of the people usually walk. Sometimes Ashley and I watch people and we try to guess if they'll step around the drawings or just walk right over them. We saw one guy who didn't notice them at first, but then when he looked down and finally saw them, he actually jumped off!

*Facing page:*
**"Accordion and Other Stuff"**

*Lynn Herr and Ashley Weir*
*Chalk on sidewalk*
*Used to be near the parking lot*

*Lynn's comment:*
*Ashley thought the music stand was a TV.*
*She also thought the whole-notes were*
*bubbles. Maybe because she was looking at*
*them upside-down. So she drew a fish and*
*an octopus, like underwater.*

Not many people use the ramps. Why does almost everyone use the steps, even though that's more difficult and boring? I even saw some people on crutches, and they also used the steps. We have to stay outside or at least not go into certain rooms, while Mrs Weir is actually working with her patients. It is a workplace, after all. But more importantly, we're supposed to Be Considerate Of Those In Need. That means we have to keep a lookout for people who might have a hard time getting through the door. Then we're supposed to open it for them. But Ashley only tries to get to the door if I'm already trying to. It has to be a race, or she doesn't feel like helping, at all. So the receptionist told us if we're going to be running around, we have to stay outside. I hate it when Ashley gets me in trouble.

We know what time Mrs Weir's lunch break is, so we go find her and she takes us somewhere. I've never been to restaurants so many times, before! Aunt Celly keeps telling me not to get used to it. She doesn't like spoiled kids. That's why she's not Ashley's biggest fan.

When Mrs Weir was a teenager, she once injured her shoulder. Ashley has already heard this story. Anyway, Teenager Sandra Weir had no idea how she got hurt, but it was really awful. She couldn't do anything at all, even with the arm that wasn't hurt, because all of the parts of the body are connected to each other, in one way or another. She had to get a shot in the joint, and then she did exercises for a while, until she was finally better. But she kept doing the exercises, ever since, so she's really healthy. Ashley is, too. They do their exercises every day at the same time.

It's their ritual. They showed me, too. And Mrs Weir let me listen to her shoulders. The regular one is just quiet, but the one that used to be injured actually makes a little crackling sound! So her old injury was really awful at the time, but if it never happened, she wouldn't have become a physical therapist. I'm supposed to keep a lookout for a Life Changing Experience of my own, from now on.

*Next page:*
**"Mrs Weir's Shoulder Noise"**

*Lynn Herr*
*Pencil on paper*
*The clinic*

*Lynn's comment:*
*At first, everyone thought it was a picture of Mrs Weir dancing or fighting, so I had to explain what it's really about.*

But on some days, like today, I just stay home with Aunt Celly, because she misses me and feels more relaxed when she knows exactly where I am. And she doesn't want to make me too much of a burden on Mrs Weir's wallet. Aunt Celly does still have to keep working at her job, though, so I really have to leave her alone when she's at her desk, unless there's an amazing reason to bother her. This is her longest project ever. The publisher sent her other novels to read, in two languages, because the one she's translating is part of a series, and some things need to come out the same in all of the books that are in the same language, or else the readers might get confused and not understand what's what and who's who. She says this is especially important, because anyone who would choose to read this series will need all the help they can get. That means the books are terrible. But that's not Aunt Celly's fault. This is just a job. And there should be other books in the series, coming out later, because the author can crank this junk out in a hurry and people keep buying it. So Aunt Celly can keep making a living and we won't be out begging on the street.

While she's working, I mostly draw pictures, organize my Collection, and talk to Colossus. Sometimes I also learn from my music book. It's pretty much impossible to put it on my music stand and turn the pages and be wearing my accordion, all at the same time, so I'll have to work something out. I hope I won't have to cut pages out of the book, to put them on the stand. That sort of thing really bothers me.

Aunt Celly's coming out of her room and stretching

out. That means she's ready to be sociable again. Sort of. She's lying on the couch. Right now in the novel, the wiseman is giving the hero a mysterious clue about where to find the third amulet, instead of just spelling it out for him plainly. I feel like Aunt Celly has already told me about scenes like this, before. Maybe wisemen have never been to the places they talk about, and that's why they can't really explain things well. That's just my idea. This time, the clue is also supposed to be a pun, but that's really hard to change into another language. Aunt Celly thought of a way to do it, though, because she's really smart. That's a good stopping point for today. This weekend, we're going to a festival with Ashley and her mom, so Aunt Celly has been working more than usual, to stay on schedule.

*Facing page:*
**"Aunt Celly's Big Job"**

*Lynn Herr*
*Pencil on paper*
*Refrigerator door*

*Lynn's comment:*
*This is pretty much exactly what's going on.*
*Except for the chair. I accidentally started*
*drawing the wrong kind, at first.*

65

~ ~ ~

Nowadays, I have lemonade for my Little Drink. I started liking it, because the vending machine at Mrs Weir's clinic has it, and Ashley's always got lots of coins and even some bills for things like that. One time, she had ten dollars! Aunt Celly still hasn't been to where Mrs Weir works, but she wants to check it out, someday.

The Weirs usually visit here, instead. It's always good to be friends with a physical therapist.

*Facing page:*
**"Massage"**

*Lynn Herr*
*Pencil on paper*
*Back pocket*

*Lynn's comment:*
*Aunt Celly was so happy when Mrs Weir gave her a massage. She said no one has touched her in years.*

I wish I took a picture of Aunt Celly's face, when I first told her what Mrs Weir's job is. Aunt Celly suddenly started having back and shoulder problems, right then and there. It was "inexplicable." Oh, I hope it's not like when Mrs Weir was a teenager and her shoulder got injured! And they do call each other "Celly" and "Sandy," like I thought they would.

I didn't know this at first, but Mrs Weir is about ten years older than Aunt Celly. So they grew up with mostly different shows and bands from each other. But they're in the same generation, pretty much. My dad was Aunt Celly's older brother, and Mrs Weir has two younger brothers, so it sort of works out. Then, if Aunt Celly ever has kids, will they be in the same generation as me? After she stopped laughing, she said at this rate, they'll probably think I'm their aunt instead of their cousin, but, yes, we should be. I've been thinking about things like this, lately, because Ashley has uncles and cousins, but I'm not sure if I do, too, or not.

Aunt Celly's thinking about it for a minute. She says "not really." That's how she likes to say "no," like when a cashier asks her if she wants to make a donation to the something-or-other charity. How about they make a donation to her, instead?

~~~

Ashley's voice for Kittyson is like the one her mom does, but not nearly as good. Other than that, she's pretty good at being Kittyson. I don't let her be Lab Master, though, because she doesn't understand him like I do. It's actually really hard to live up to him, since he's so smart about science and he's such a gentleman. I've got his autograph in my Collection. His handwriting is as handsome and careful as he is. And that's saying a lot! Ashley's not allowed to touch it. I have Kittyson's autograph, too, but only because it also came with the membership package. He can't really tell uppercase from lowercase. What a travesty! I completely understand why Lab Master can't stand him. One thing I don't get about Lab Master, though, is why he's not married. Most men of his age and academic standing are, right?

*Next two pages:*
**"Lab Master at Home"**

*Lynn Herr*
*Pencil on paper*
*~~The Collection~~  Aunt Celly's room!*

*Lynn's comment:*
*Aunt Celly loves this one.*

Mrs Weir has been in Aunt Celly's room for an hour, already. I can't really guess what they're talking about. Adults don't really play, so pretty much all they do is talk. Or they play by talking. That's why adults watch movies with a lot of conversations. Aunt Celly and Mrs Weir could be talking about anything, because they're regular-aged adults instead of elderly ones. Every time I hear old people talking to each other, like in a restaurant or somewhere, it's about gross health stuff no one wants to hear while eating, or it's about things from a very long time ago that don't matter anymore. Doesn't that get boring? Actually, now that I think about it, Mrs Weir also talks about medical stuff a lot. That's alright, though, because it's mostly about how muscles and bones are connected, instead of about fixing guts and kidneys that don't work anymore.

But I'm going to be a scientist when I grow up, so I might have to learn a lot about all of that sort of thing. I used to think I wanted to be a veterinarian. Because of Colossus. Then I could take care of animals for a living, and whenever I'll introduce myself as a veterinarian, everyone will be amazed and they'll want to be my friend. I once saw that happen in real life. Really, though, I think I'll go into chemistry, or make proteins, or do something else like that.

~ ~ ~

It's hard to sleep, from being so excited about the festival. This must be the first time I've been awake late enough to see Colossus come in and go to his bed on my floor. He's also going to the festival, tomorrow. It's pretty hot outside nowadays, so we won't bring his sweater.

~~~

We haven't heard of any of the bands on the flier. I hope I'll like them, anyway. The flier also has a map in it. I'm normally good at this sort of thing, but it's a map of the festival grounds, instead of how to get to the festival, in the first place. The directions are just explained with words. Aunt Celly gets headaches from trying to read things inside the car while it's moving, but road signs outside of the car are just fine for her. She's the navigator on the trip, so she has to look out for the turns. Mrs Weir uses the horn a lot, but also just barely. She just taps it, to tell other drivers to go ahead. I can tell it's driving Aunt Celly crazy. She keeps glancing back at me, and it's hard for me not to laugh. Poor Colossus, he really isn't used to riding in cars. I'm holding him in my lap, so he won't shift around so much. We had to bring his leash, because it'll be a public festival outside. There might be other dogs there. (No one ever brings pet cats anywhere, though.) He gets tired easily, especially in weather like this, so we'll probably have to carry him for a lot of the time. For some reason, most festivals are during the hottest season of the year. Aunt Celly says it's a scam to sell cold drinks at inflated prices to a captive audience. Even Mrs Weir thinks festival food is expensive, so we filled up at a restaurant, beforehand.

Colossus is really popular at the festival. People keep petting him and baby-talking to him. Maybe the festival should have put a picture of Colossus in the flier. Everyone thinks that's a good joke.

There are a lot of kilts here. Yes, I know what those are. Aunt Celly and Mrs Weir are talking quietly to each other. Ashley was sneaking around and she says she heard what they said, but she won't tell me what it was. The festival is pretty loud, after all, so maybe she didn't actually hear their whispering. Or maybe she did. All I know is, Aunt Celly is getting mighty fed up with Ashley trying to spy on them.

*Facing page:*
**"Your Aunt is Mean"**

*Ashley Weir*
*Pen on paper*
*Undisclosed location in Ashley's room*

*Lynn's comment:*
*Ashley says Aunt Celly is always angry at her but never at me or Colossus. Yeah.*

It looked like Aunt Celly and one of the guys in a kilt were getting to be friends. She pointed me out and told him I'm her niece. He said "that's cool." Kind of a weird thing to say. They talked for a few more minutes. After that, Aunt Celly told me she was going to keep working the room for a while longer. It's actually a really big tent, though, not a room. I'm going back to our table, to check on Colossus. Some people are taking a picture with him.

Ashley won't tell me what she heard Aunt Celly and the guys in the tent talking about. Again, with this!? She got busted after a little while, anyway, so she probably didn't overhear much.

It's kind of like being in a movie or a play, because of the costumes and the actors. But most of the people look normal, like us. I didn't know we could have dressed up. I don't have my Lab Master costume yet, anyway. Maybe this is where movies and plays get their stuff from. The shops mostly sell special things I never see in real life. Some of the clothes and tools are old-fashioned. A long time ago, people used to drink from cow horns that can't even stand up on tables. It must have been a hard life. Also, because of all the fighting. There were battles and wars, all the time. Now there's a combat lesson going on, but those swords are just made of wood, so the fighters won't really kill each other. They do have real metal swords, too, but I won't go near them. Because they're so expensive. Ashley tried to pick one up, but she said it weighed a ton. The sword teacher defeated a watermelon and gave us pieces of it. I shared mine with Aunt Celly. We took turns with it. Ashley also shared hers with her mom, but they split it completely in half, first. Maybe they're afraid of germs.

This has got to be the weirdest thing I ever saw. Ashley's dancing around like crazy! Or is it even really dancing? Why isn't she getting tired? Even Aunt Celly doesn't know what she's seeing. Ashley did stop for a little while, though, while the band was deciding what song to play next. Some older girls are dancing in a circle, more like normal humans, and they let Ashley in. I think she was trying to get their attention, in the first place. Even when the band went away, Ashley still wasn't tired. She just stopped dancing and acted like nothing happened. And as soon as she wasn't dancing anymore, I couldn't even remember what it looked like. That's how strange the whole thing was. Sometimes it's like I don't even know who she is.

We're starting to get hungry at the festival, so it's time to leave. Colossus is really tired, anyway, from making so many friends. I thought Aunt Celly did pretty well at it, too, since she was talking to lots of guys, but she says she's leaving empty-handed. Yeah, we didn't buy any souvenirs.

Of course, now Ashley gets tired! She's completely conked out in the car. Colossus is, too, but that's normal for him. I guess he got used to riding in the car.

That's so weird, how I just woke up in front of my house. I didn't realize I fell asleep. It's not very late, but all I want to do is go right to bed. This must be how Colossus feels, all the time.

~~~

I'm happy for Aunt Celly. Now she's got Mrs Weir as a close friend and they trust each other with everything. I think that's better in some ways than only having "old friends" who are far away. Aunt Celly won't stop being old friends with them, but now she doesn't have to expect much of anything from them anymore, either. Now it can just be a whenever-or-not kind of thing with them, and that's okay. I'm starting to think having close friends is sometimes hard, because of missing them when they're somewhere else. I thought it was just supposed to always be good. Aunt Celly says really up-and-down things like this make people age in a hurry, from stress, so I should take it easy and embrace boredom while I still can.

*Facing page:*
***"Ancient Treasure Map"***

*Ashley Weir just by herself*
*Pen and lighter on paper*
*Well hidden*

*Lynn's comment:*
*Ashley got a lighter from somewhere and tried Aunt Celly's trick for making paper look old. It got out of hand.*

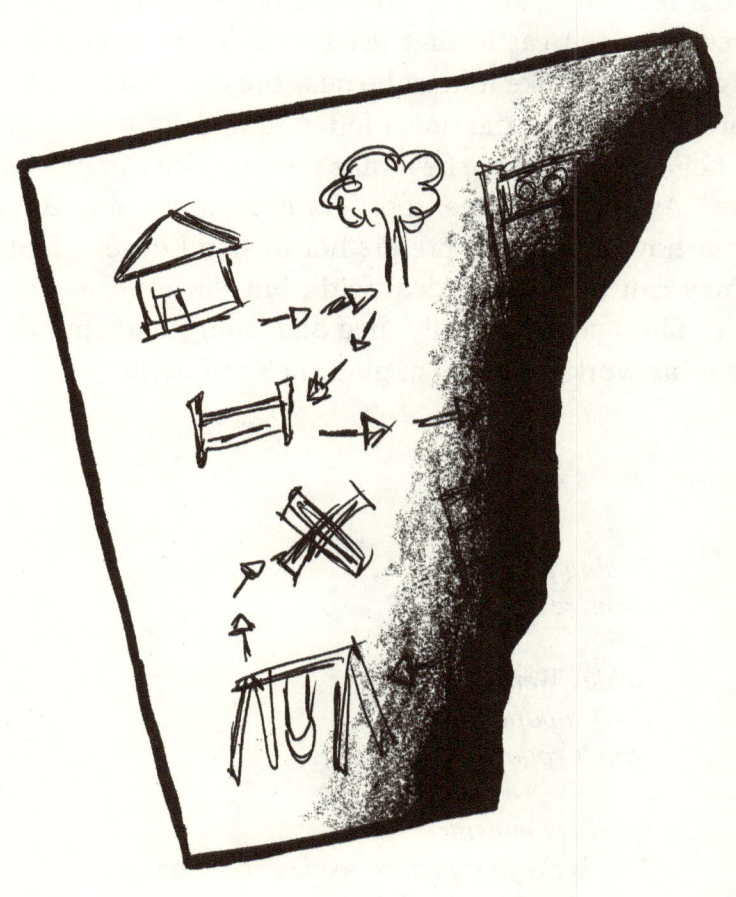

I got an update on Aunt Celly's work. The hero in the novel found the third amulet and also got the magic sword. I wonder if it's like the ones from a few days ago, at the festival. Anyway, now the hero can fight the evil sorcerer in the castle that used to belong to the rightful king. It sounds like it must be near the end, but there's still more than half of the novel left. Aunt Celly is despairing for her career. I hope she'll take it easy, until Mrs Weir gets here. Ashley will come, too. I'm not supposed to tell her about how Aunt Celly prefers her in small doses. I get it. Ashley can be hard to deal with, but I'm used to her, by now. She's actually really nice and funny, and she makes lots of artwork for me. I'm glad she's my friend.

*Facing page:*
**"You're My Friend"**

*Ashley Weir*
*Pen on paper*
*Lynn's room*

*Lynn's comment:*
*This is the first picture Ashley ever drew for me. It was really nice of her.*

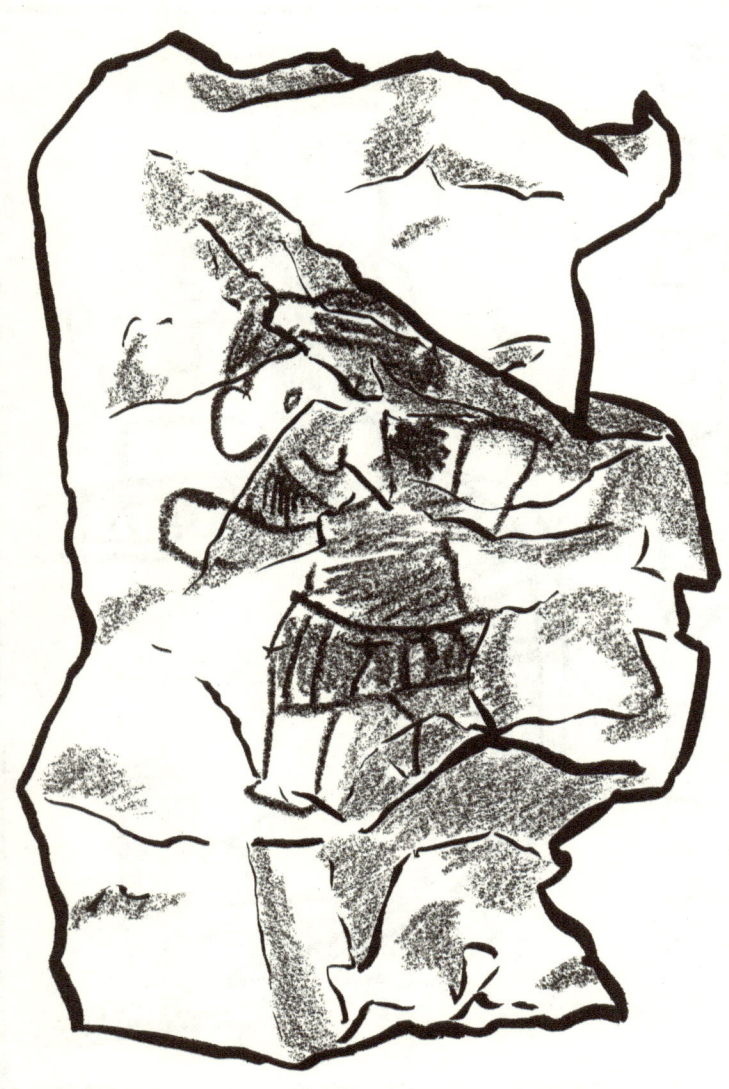

~ ~ ~

I hope I never see that stupid Ashley Weir ever again!

*Facing page:*
**"(Name Redacted)"**

*Lynn Herr*
*Pencil on paper*
*Trashcan*

*Lynn's comment:*
*Ashley's not my friend anymore and now I*
*hate her.*

Aunt Celly says my dad's little accordion isn't actually broken, because nothing important got knocked loose and the scratch doesn't change how it sounds. Don't I know when my own stuff is wrecked!? Aunt Celly doesn't even play music anymore, so what does she know!?

I'm really sorry I thought something so mean about Aunt Celly. That was a terrible thing for me to do. Now I feel even worse than I already did. It's weird, feeling so many different things at the same time. Angry at Ashley for dropping my stuff that I told her not to even touch at all, and sad that I got upset at Aunt Celly for no reason, and also happy that she always takes such good care of me. She's letting me cool down for a while, until I feel like talking.

We didn't do Little Drinks tonight, since it was already pretty late, but we did talk about things. Sometimes Aunt Celly feels different things at the same time, too. Or she even has different feelings about one same thing. She was scared about becoming my godmother when I was a baby, but she's also happy she did. I am, too. So now I feel a lot better. But Ashley still may not come over, ever again!

~~~

Not sure why I woke up. I don't remember having a bad dream. Or any dream at all. But something's weird.

It's really quiet. That's what's weird. I don't hear Colossus snorting. Oh, because he's not even in my room. Then he must still be in the living room.

Yeah.

It's been a whole minute. I'm supposed to try to wake him up.

It's not working.

~~~

Aunt Celly is really amazing. She knew everything to do. We've talked before, about how this was going to happen someday, so I was supposed to be ready for it. But I don't think I was. I wish I could've helped. Aunt Celly's resting now, and keeping me warm. I've never been outside, this early in the morning. It makes the backyard look strange.

Before I was born, Colossus belonged to my dad. When Aunt Celly started taking care of me, Colossus came along with the deal. So he was a bonus. I can't remember a time before I knew him.

So maybe no one completely understands passing away. Even still, what is it? Colossus is just gone? I know where he is, but also he's not really there anymore. So his life is gone, then. His body got too old and couldn't work anymore. Okay...? But I'm not sure that's really what I'm asking about. Maybe I'm wording it wrong. This whole thing has to make sense, somehow.

~~~

Huh. Aunt Celly suddenly wants to read some "Lab

Master and Kittyson" issues with me. I used to wonder if she secretly didn't like them very much, but now she looks excited about it. I must've gotten used to the voices Mrs Weir does. She's so nice. It's no wonder Aunt Celly likes her so much. But I can't figure out how Ashley turned out to be such a jerk. Doesn't she get everything she wants?

I don't know yet what happens next in the novel, because Aunt Celly didn't work on it today. I got to spend the whole day with her. And I got to choose dinner. That almost never happens.

~ ~ ~

Can Colossus still hear me? Should I not talk to him anymore? I'll ask Aunt Celly about it, in the morning.

*Facing page:*
**"I Don't Know"**

*Lynn Herr*
*Pencil on paper*
*Lynn's room*

*Lynn's comment:*
*This whole thing is very confusing.*

~~~

She wasn't kidding about death being a big mystery. It's age-old. That means people have wondered about it for as long as there have been people in the world. And no one at all has figured it out? Because no one can die and then come back to life and talk about what it was like to be dead. Except some people say they know all about it, anyway, and they'll lie about anything, and I shouldn't buy what they're selling. That's a really good Pearl of Wisdom. Even a lot of grown-ups don't know that one. Aunt Celly has probably known this sort of thing for a long time already, so she's doing alright. But I'm just now learning it, so I'm still mixed up about things.

My birthday is still a whole month away. That's a long time. Aunt Celly is bringing it up so early, just because she's trying to cheer me up. But I don't feel like thinking about my birthday. I guess because it should be a happy time, but Colossus will still be gone. And Ashley's not my friend anymore, so it'll be a sad time with just me and Aunt Celly by ourselves.

And I can't believe how alright Aunt Celly is about Colossus dying. I must have loved him a lot more than... No. Not that sort of thing again. That's a terrible thing to think. I know Aunt Celly loved Colossus, too. Just as much as I did. She even knew him a lot longer than I did. She says its okay for me to cry, if I have to, even if she doesn't.

It was so hard to just tell Aunt Celly how sad I am. In her own way, she also misses Colossus, even if it doesn't look like it.  She just wanted to be strong for me, so I wouldn't get scared from worrying about her.  That meant she was trying to keep it on the inside and work it out for herself, first.  After all these years of taking care of Colossus, Aunt Celly still always thought of him as her brother's dog, instead of her own.  Like how Aunt Celly takes care of me, even though I'm a niece instead of a daughter to her, Colossus was like a nephew version of a pet.  Or maybe I'm just not explaining it well.  What I mean is, to Aunt Celly, it was like we were only borrowing Colossus for a while.  But once he died, Aunt Celly started thinking he really was ours, after all.  So this whole thing is very mixed up for her, too, but not in the same way as it is for me.

Ashley and her mom liked Colossus, too.  Of course, anyone would have.  Even strangers did.  But the Weirs don't know about Colossus passing away.  Aunt Celly will tell Mrs Weir about it, but I have to be a big girl and tell Ashley, myself.  I hate it when I have to be a big girl.  Because it always means doing something I don't want to.  But, alright.  I guess I can manage it.  I do kind of miss Ashley, after all.

*Facing page:*
**"Happy Birthday, Lynn!"**

*Ashley Weir*
*Pen on two pieces of paper*
*A wall in Lynn's room*

*Lynn's comment:*
*Ashley made this for my birthday. That's
why she's holding a present, at the end.
There's a neat trick where the drawing is
always upside-down and downside-up, at the
same time. So I sometimes flip it around and
hang it up the other way.*

# 3:

# Autumn

Our costumes only have to hold up for tonight, and next year, we might be too big for the shirts and pants. Aunt Celly swore she'll never again use her sewing machine for evil. But no way, either, was she about to pay retail price for stuff I'll only wear once. I wasn't sure if the Lab Master costume means I'm supposed to also act like him. I guess not, since Ashley's just talking like normal, instead of doing her crummy Kittyson voice. It's weird that the tie makes me feel smarter. It's an essential part of the outfit. Lab Master never appears in public without one. Kittyson probably would, though. Because he's a slob. And not many people notice this, but Lab Master uses special ties that make the design on the flap-part slant in the same direction as on the knot-part. When the lines go in opposite directions, like on normal ties, it looks wrong to me.

I have actually gone trick-or-treating before. Colossus used to come along with a costume of his own, because Aunt Celly said it would get me a bigger haul from the neighborhood. Before that, when I was really little, Aunt Celly and I once did Hallowe'en at home, but I didn't understand the ghost was just Aunt Celly in a costume. Because I was too young. That was the most scared I ever was. After that, we started doing Hallowe'en more like normal people, to avoid traumatizing me anymore.

*Facing page:*
**"Hallowe'en"**

*Lynn Herr*
*Pencil on paper*
*Ashley's room*

*Lynn's comment:*
*We got lots of good stuff. I don't know if*
*anyone recognized our costumes, though.*

Some of the neighbors' houses are decorated with neat stuff like gravestones and spiderwebs and skeletons. Mine isn't. Aunt Celly isn't about to spend her hard-earned money on junk like that, when we can just look at other people's set-ups for free. The material for our costumes was expensive enough. We had a coupon for fifty-percent-off, but when we got to the fabric store, everything was already ten-percent-off, so that meant we couldn't use the coupon, because of a stipulation. Aunt Celly said it was a scam to get people into the store, and she almost called off the whole thing. But Mrs Weir ended up paying for everything, and she's got lots of money, so I'm not sure why Aunt Celly stayed mad about it for so long. We can't even pass by that store anymore without her trying to hex it.

Hallowe'en is supposed to be pretend-scary just for fun, not actual-scary, right? But there's one neighborhood guy who's dressed up like a life-sized monster decoration and sits on the front step of his house, and when anyone gets close, he suddenly moves and scares them for real. I mean, they actually scream! How's that supposed to be fun? Ashley and I have been watching this for a few minutes. I can't believe she actually wants us to go there. No way am I getting near that place!

That was the most scared I ever was. Even though I knew he would move. He waited so long, though, I thought he might not, but then he did. I'd better find where Ashley ran away to.

I got some pretty good stuff, tonight. Ashley wants to trade something of hers for my avocado. Two cherry tomatoes, really!? It's worth at least three. Okay then. She doesn't want my plantain, thankfully, but I'm sure she'd trade her raisins for my baby carrots. She likes crunchy food, probably because it's loud and makes people notice her. And she can't eat her grapefruit, because she's allergic, so she'll have to take anything at all for it. Oh, but then she'd probably want a bonus for the next trade, so I'd better give her the whole pack of pretzels, to keep things fair. And we still haven't payed the Aunt Celly Tax, yet.

We'll have to wait until later for Aunt Celly to dig through our haul and claim her tribute, though, since she's busy watching a scary movie, right now. I caught just a little bit of it on accident, when we got back. Ugh! Just awful. Adults are so weird. Their smoking stinks and makes kisses gross, and their drinks taste like fire and make people sick, and their movies are either just a bunch of talking for a long time or people doing illegal crimes and shooting guns. So what I can't figure out is how stuff for kids is all made by adults, but it's still good, anyway.

~ ~ ~

The main difference between this grade and last one is my new homeroom. It's in a hallway I didn't know about, before. Also, I have a new homeroom teacher, of course. He's alright. Aunt Celly says that's how to make a clean break, so I'm not supposed to share her weird stories anymore. The other thing is, now I have to go to more different classrooms, instead of other teachers coming to my homeroom. It's a real pain. I heard the older kids have to move for every single class, going all over the building and even to the creepy trailers out back. And even worse, while they're away from their homeroom, other students go in there and sit at their desks! I'm going to be really upset, if that's true. So, actually, there are a lot of main differences from last grade.

*Facing page:*
***"Accordion Vest"***

*Celesta Herr*
*Patch and buttons on clearance vest*
*Lynn's dresser*

*Lynn's comment:*
*Now it's finally the right weather, so I can wear this. Everyone at school is really impressed.*

Ashley and I didn't end up in the same homeroom. That's pretty much the only thing that didn't change. So I can still only see her on the bus, at Lunch Time, at Free Play Time, after school, and on weekends and vacations. I don't think that's fair. But this weekend will have a No School Holiday next to it, and I'll sort of be living in Ashley's house until things get back to normal. I slept over there a few times during summer vacation, so that's not weird, but I do think it'll be strange how I might not even get to see Aunt Celly at all for a day or two. I can't remember anything like that, before, because I was very little when she got me.

No one remembers being a baby or a toddler, but everyone older than that must have been one. I've seen a few pictures of myself from when I was really small. It's like looking at someone else. Maybe the reason people don't remember being very little is, if they did, they would be mortified about how messy and whiny they were. Aunt Celly's idea is about how really little kids have no idea what's happening even at the time, so it's no wonder they can't remember those things later. Aunt Celly would know a lot more about this than I would, because she has life experience and I don't.

The earliest thing I can remember is seeing a frog in the backyard. It was getting dark outside, and maybe it had stopped raining a little while ago, but I'm pretty sure it wasn't coming down at the time. In the memory, the frog had also shown up the night before in the same spot, but I don't actually remember that first night at all. It was my same back yard as now. Probably. Otherwise, I don't know where it would have been. So I guess Aunt Celly was there, and she was the one who told me it was the frog's second visit. I don't remember the voice, or the exact words. Just an explanation about the frog.

My other earliest memory is about the big wrinkles on Colossus's back. It's called the nape of the neck. Sometimes people pick up cats by the nape of the neck, but that looks like an awful thing to do, even though it's a cat. I mean, when mother-cats carry their kittens like that, it's alright. They're supposed to. Anyway, I don't remember anything actually happening in that memory about the wrinkles. It's more like just a close-up picture.

I asked Aunt Celly, because this sort of thing is what Little Drinks is for, and I'd better go ahead and use up all of my questions. One of her earliest memories is about being in an indoor swimming pool and seeing a big painting of a cartoon alligator (or maybe a crocodile) on the wall. It was probably wearing sunglasses. Aunt Celly is mostly sure about that detail, but not completely, and now her brain can't tell if she really saw sunglasses on the alligator (crocodile?) or if she just imagined that part. Anyway, she can't remember what the water in the pool was like, even though swimming pool water is always terribly cold. And she has no idea where the place was. Maybe earliest memories don't have to mean anything special. There's no rule about it.

Little Drinks does have rules, though. I may ask anything I want, as long as I think I'm ready to hear the answer. So I have to be thoughtful about my questions.

And if Aunt Celly does answer it, she has to tell me the truth, or at least what she thinks is true. But if she just can't answer or doesn't want to, maybe because she really has no idea or I'm not old enough for it, then she has to tell me so. It happens, sometimes. The same rules also work the other way around, but Aunt Celly doesn't ask me very much during Little Drinks. I mean, really, what Pearl of Wisdom could I give her? Also, Aunt Celly is my legal guardian, so she has "veto power." That means she can make me answer an Important Question, even if I really don't want to. She has to actually call it "an Important Question." That's what makes it official. And it might happen at any time, not just during Little Drinks. It's for my safety and other serious things like that. So if Aunt Celly ever needs the details of something, I absolutely have to tell her the truth, even if it's embarrassing or something's my fault. For real, no joking around. I promised. But I almost never get Important Questioned, because I'm cooperative and low-maintenance.

~~~

It's the last day before the long weekend. The teachers are mostly just showing videos. Even the school doesn't want to be open today. I can tell, because the cafeteria is serving sack-lunches instead of real ones. That's why it's worth lugging my lunchbox around, every day. Just in case. Ashley once dared me to try eating one of the peanut butter sandwiches from a sack left on our table. I didn't really have to chew it much, but it was the only time I ever actually felt a bite of food all the way down in my chest. I thought it would never get to my stomach. This time, though, I'll be ready for it, and I'll make sure Ashley tries it, too. In fact, she'll have to go first! And I finally remembered to bring up that bulletin board in the hallway. The one with alphabet letters in the math problems. What in the world is "three A equals fifteen" supposed to mean!? Ashley's got no idea, either. She never even noticed that bulletin board, but now she wants to hear all about it. Or maybe she's just stalling for time. In another few minutes, Lunch Time will be over, so Ashley won't have to try the sack-sandwich I found for her.

*Next page:*
**"Don't Eat the Sack-Lunch Sandwich"**

*Lynn Herr and Ashley Weir*
*Pencil and pen on paper*
*Ashley's desk*

*Lynn's comment:*
*I drew the sandwich, then Ashley drew everything else. She's pretty good at making stuff up.*

I do really like nature documentaries, but there's just no way I can focus on this one right now. I can tell this business with the letters in the numbers will keep bugging me until someone explains what it's all about. The teacher doesn't look very busy, just pacing around and looking out the window, so I could ask him.

Ugh. I was happier with not knowing. The letters actually mean numbers. But they can't look like numbers, because no one knows what numbers they should be. So I think they should be question marks, instead. But no, they're letters, and they could be any letters. It doesn't matter which ones. So the "a" up there probably has nothing to do with the "a" on the other side of the board. This whole nonsense started because someone got the idea to move the answer into the question-side, and to put something else on the answer-side. Well, if I already know what something-do-whatever-something equals, then isn't the problem already solved? Except the do-something parts don't work like they used to. So "x" doesn't mean "times" anymore. It's just a letter now, like spelling words. But in math, that means its actually a number. And now to do "times," numbers or letters (or whatever they're supposed to be now) are just put next to each other, and "plus" still works the same but "minus" only sometimes does, and I don't even want to talk about "divided by." This is the worst thing I ever heard of. At least I don't have to learn this stuff for real, yet. Or maybe it will get canceled, by the time I'm old enough. For now, though, I'm not sure how I'll explain it to Ashley.

There was a fire alarm. We always get told ahead of time about drills, so I thought this time might be the real thing. When we got outside, there was already a firetruck parked in front of the school and some firefighters were just standing around. I thought they just got there too fast, and had to wait for everyone to come out, before fighting the fire. But it really was a drill, after all. The firefighters did a show. It was kind of funny. They made the principal spray a fire extinguisher at a fire in a big tub, but the flames kept coming back after a few seconds, so he kept trying harder. Ashley snuck over to me for a minute and said they were going to set someone on fire for the finale of the show, like a movie stunt. I kept waiting, but it didn't happen. I was glad, actually.

The firefighting show was so long, there isn't enough time left to finish the last video. So there's pretty much a party going on in the classroom, instead. I'm just waiting until the bus ride home, to tell Ashley what I found out about the letters and numbers.

Wow. Lunch Time was only a few hours ago, and Ashley already forgot all about the bulletin board I mentioned. I knew she wasn't really listening!

~~~

I don't usually miss Aunt Celly during sleep-overs, but I do, this time. It's not a regular one. She's not sure anymore how many days I'll be at the Weirs' house. Probably still the whole long weekend. And maybe even for a few school days afterward! That'll be really weird. Anyway, I'm supposed to take it easy, and not give Mrs Weir a hard time.

So there's no Little Drinks tonight. No big deal. Ashley and her mom don't really do anything like that at home. Of course, I know it's an Aunt Celly Invention, and even she sometimes decides to give it a rest. When Ashley spent a few nights at my house, last summer, we didn't try to do Little Drinks. Because Aunt Celly wouldn't have wanted to answer the kind of questions Ashley would want to ask. It would have been "pass," "pass," "pass" every time. And I figured Ashley would argue over the rules and want exceptions just for herself, and I'm sure she would have whined and complained about Aunt Celly's "unfair" veto power. Not worth the stress! Just getting Ashley to eat Aunt Celly's cooking was hard enough.

Some of my ideas about what's wrong with Ashley aren't just mine. Most of them, actually. I'll try to remember the exact phrases Aunt Celly used. I think Ashley is just accustomed to all of her own stuff and how her family does everything, and she thinks only those things are the right ones. So anything different from that is weird and wrong to her. She can't get used to new things that are different until she forgets they once used to be new and strange. That's why she's so fussy and makes life difficult for everyone. And even though she's usually loud and not very careful about much of anything, she's also delicate and doesn't know how easy she has it. Aunt Celly has a fantasy about ditching her in a foreign country, to make her "get over herself real fast." Of course, Aunt Celly would never really do that sort of thing. Plane tickets cost a fortune.

That reminds me of something. One time, an old friend sent Aunt Celly a package from overseas. It took two months to arrive! Because the idiot post office over there put it on a ship instead of on a plane, even though it was just a normal-sized box. Another time, Aunt Celly sent the old friend a package. She paid enough to make sure it would get there in a week or two, and it did, but then the post office over there made the old friend pay money to get her own package. What a racket! But, anyway, I got distracted.

Aunt Celly and I get on this topic a lot, because understanding Ashley helps Aunt Celly deal with her. So maybe they're finally starting to warm up to each other.

*Facing page:*
**"Celly and Ashley are Cool"**

*Ashley Weir*
*Pen on paper*
*Ashley's desk at school*

*Lynn's comment:*
*I swear, nothing like this ever happened!*

At least Aunt Celly is happy for me, that I have my first ever best friend. Even though it's Ashley. So of course, I do really like her a lot, but I don't like everything about her. She sometimes makes things up and then acts like they're true. It's not always lying, though. Maybe sometimes she thinks they really are true, but other times, she knows they're not. Aunt Celly says lying isn't always about tricking people. That's sometimes just a by-product of the fabrication process. (That was one of the exact phrases.) Another reason for lying is more about taking control and feeling strong. So to tell a lie for that reason, a person has to already feel helpless or weak. How sad! So it helps Aunt Celly to feel sorry for Ashley instead of just getting angry at her all the time, like before. That's a little better, I guess. But I do wish they would get along for real, instead of just getting on each other's nerves.

It's weird, but also nice, how quiet Ashley is when she sleeps. Just regular breathing, and sometimes what sounds a bit like whispering a word or two. She doesn't even fidget around. She just picks a pose and stays that way. She's so conked out, she's not even waking up from me and her mom talking right here. Mrs Weir says Ashley burns through every bit of energy from being awake to the fullest, and that's why she's so peaceful while she's asleep and also falls asleep so easily. Because she wears herself out all the time and has to re-charge from zero.

Mrs Weir says I'm different, though. I tend to save my energy for the long haul and I usually still have some left over at night. So that's why it takes so long for me to fall asleep. Huh. I never thought about it, like that. My idea was it's because I keep thinking about things instead of just relaxing. Oh, what do I think about? Things that happened in the daytime. What they mean. What I think about them. Mrs Weir says I'm very thoughtful. And life is endlessly full of things to wonder about and figure out, so I'll never need to be bored.

I like how Mrs Weir tucks me in. It makes me think she really likes being a mom. Aunt Celly once told me the exact same thing about her, but I couldn't understand what that meant. It made being a mom sound like a hobby. I think what Aunt Celly meant, though, is some people feel happy about taking care of kids. Any kids. Aunt Celly doesn't. She's just glad to take care of me. Just me. Because I appreciate everything she does for me, just like she hopes I do.

*Next page:*
**"Li'l Lynn"**

*Celesta and Lynn Herr*
*Color-paper and glue*
*Aunt Celly's wall*

*Lynn's comment:*
*We made this artwork of me, to put near*
*Aunt Celly's desk. She says it helps her get*
*back to work.*

~~~

Today, Mrs Weir taught me lots of games. Ashley already knows all of them. She also cheats at all of them. Mrs Weir is smart, so she can sometimes guess what cards we probably have left, but Ashley just peeks. It's so obvious, too. Maybe it makes the games more fun, to guess how Ashley's cheating and to try catching her red-handed. One time, she still had an Ace from the last game. It was in her lap. Mrs Weir discovered that one, because she's a lot taller than me. Another time, Ashley went to the kitchen for something and took her hand with her. I busted her swapping out cards from a secret stash in a cabinet. Now we have to go through every deck in the house and find out what's missing or if there are too many of something in them.

Homework is fine, as long as it's literature. Usually, anyway. My reading assignment for the long weekend is about a prince who is very rich, but he's also miserable. The king wants to cheer him up, so he gives him more stuff, but the prince still doesn't feel any better. Then a wiseman (uh-oh!) tells the king to find the happiest man in the world, take his shirt, and give it to the prince. Okay, sure. That's just the kind of weird advice a wiseman would give. So the king finds a happy person, but doesn't take his shirt. It was because the happy person wanted to be happier than he already was. That meant he wasn't already the happiest. Then the same thing happens again. Now the king is really worried. Then he finds a poor farmer who likes being a poor farmer just fine, but this guy doesn't even have a shirt. A jacket, but not a shirt. The jacket doesn't count. So that's it. The story's over.

*Facing page:*
**"The King Talks to the Farmer"**

*Lynn Herr*
*Pencil on paper*
*Ashley's house*

*Lynn's comment:*
*This is from my reading assignment. It's*
*when the king was talking to the farmer.*
*The reason it looks so much better than most*
*of my drawings is I tried to copy the real*
*artwork from the book.*

I think the moral is about how having less stuff makes people feel happier, but I'm not so sure about that. There's a ton of stuff I want. I just feel weird asking Aunt Celly for it. Her job doesn't pay a whole lot, even though she went to college for it. In fact, she's still paying for college! That's a good chunk of change, every month, just gone forever.

A lot of the stuff I wish I could have, Ashley's already got in her room. It's one of my favorite places. She's got pretty much everything from the ads in the "Lab Master and Kittyson" issues. Even the complete set of tapes. It drives me crazy, though, how she won't put them in order! It's not like the numbers are tiny or hidden away somewhere. She even puts some of the tapes backward into the boxes. The label is obviously supposed to be on the same side as the front cover. I'm tired of having to fix this, every time.

*Next 3 pages:*
**"Supposed to be just Lab Master"**

*Lynn Herr and Ashley Weir*
*Chalk on board*
*Ashley's room*

*Lynn's comment:*
*I started the story, then Ashley continued it,*
*then I finished it.*

~~~

Aunt Celly is here! I'm really happy, especially since I thought she might not be able to visit. It's already pretty late, though. Tonight is the first time we're doing Little Drinks here. Aunt Celly decided to. She insisted. And we have to let Ashley and her mom join in, since this is their house, and we're just guests. So I'm explaining the rules to them. Mrs Weir gets the idea, just fine. She says it sounds neat. Especially because of being granted veto power of her own. Maybe we should have told her about all of this, sooner. But Ashley... Ugh.

No, Little Drinks isn't really about being thirsty.

Yes, you may have a big cup, if you don't want a little one.

No, you're supposed to get just a little bit of juice, since it's late.

Yes, you may have more than that, if your mom says it's okay.

No, you may not have what the adults are drinking.

Yes, I'm sure.

No, you don't get to ask Important Questions of your own, even if you make them official.

For crying out loud! May Ashley be excused, then? Little Drinks isn't supposed to be nearly so complicated.

My question tonight is one I didn't get to ask, last night. It's about why teachers in higher grades only teach one subject, but the students are still supposed to learn every subject. Mrs Weir says it's good for everyone to start learning about all kinds of different subjects when they're young, so they can end up picking some of those things to still be good at when they're older. If kids never knew about those things, in the first place, they couldn't decide if they like them or not. So it's a way of trying stuff out. That makes sense.

It's not like Aunt Celly's answer, though. She says teachers, like all adults, already went through the system of being a student and having to learn a whole bunch of subjects in school. But in real life, the most complicated parts of a subject are only useful to people who end up making money from knowing it, and that's not many people. So everyone mostly forgets the rest of the most complicated stuff, like they never even learned it at all. It's no different with teachers. They're just the adults who went back into the same system, but from the tail end of it, so now they're the employees instead of the customers. They know the system is still throwing everything at the wall and not much sticks. Even still, adults have to make a living somehow, and keeping kids in school means some adults can get paid from teaching the students, and the students' parents are freed up to have jobs of their own. Not very romantic, but that's how it all works. Hmm.

No, Ashley, you don't have to answer the question, too.

But yes, you may, if you want to.

Ashley's answer is about how teachers "don't get how things really are." She says teachers think each subject is the only one, so they can't understand about students having to learn a bunch of other ones, too. And that's for every subject, so it gets just ridiculous after a while. I guess that must be how it feels, to her. Not really to me, though, since I'm good at most subjects, but she's not.

I thought all of the answers were pretty interesting. Mrs Weir said it was because I had asked an interesting question.

*Facing page:*
**"Little Drinks with the Weirs"**

*Lynn Herr*
*Pencil on paper*
*Ashley's house*

*Lynn's comment:*
*This was just before Ashley ruined everything.*

When it was Ashley's turn to ask something, she had a question just for Aunt Celly, but wouldn't even say what it was! Because she was sure Aunt Celly wouldn't answer it, anyway. So then I really wanted to know what it was, but no one could get it out of her. That's not how Little Drinks is supposed to work! It's give-an-answer, not guess-a-question. That was pretty much the end of it. Fine with me!

Aunt Celly is spending the night here. That's another first, for tonight. She doesn't want to go home without me and be lonely, I think. It's so cozy here with her. We talked about Colossus. I still miss him, and I'm still sad he's gone, but it does feel like it was a long time ago. So it's not as bad as it used to be. And I still don't want a new dog. It wouldn't feel right.

~~~

Ashley asked for more breakfast but then barely ate any of it. I can't believe Aunt Celly didn't say anything about it, or at least roll her eyes. Instead, she just watched. That's unheard of.

I'm really not sure what's going on with her. I have an idea, though. I think she's doing an important rush job at home for a lot of money, and maybe the story is the kind she can't tell me about until I'm older, like that one time, and she needs complete concentration. So I can't be there, or else I might bother her, but she doesn't want me to know I might mess up her project, because I would feel bad about it, even if I didn't do anything. But she still has to sometimes take breaks for sleeping, and she misses me, and that's why she'll try to visit again, tonight. That's my idea. Aunt Celly didn't tell me if it's right or not. I just have to stay the course and not pick up any habits from Ashley. That's fine. I'll try to think of a new idea to ask Aunt Celly about, whenever she gets back. I should have all day.

Of course, Ashley hasn't even thought about starting her reading assignment, yet. Hers is different from mine, because we're not in the same class. She got a pretty good story. It's about two woodcutters. I thought the word was "woodman," but that's not what's in this book. Anyway, it's a fairy-tale kind of job, sort of like a lumberjack. I don't think there really are woodcutters anymore. Because how could a guy with just an axe make a living from chopping down trees, when now there are machines doing that a lot better? Anyway, the two woodcutters in the story don't know each other. They don't even meet. It's about them dropping their axes into a pond, on accident. Just not at the same time. They're both really upset about the accidents, and they don't know what to do next. Then a fairy appears from the pond and asks them about what happened. First, she shows them a really expensive axe made of gold. Their real ones were cheap and old, though. Second, she shows them their real axes. One of the woodcutters decides to tell the truth instead of being greedy, so the fairy gives him the expensive axe, as a reward. She also gives him his regular one back, even though he could just sell the golden one and never have to work again. Anyway, the other woodcutter lies, because he just wants to get rich, no matter what. He says the golden one is his, and he pretends not to recognize his actual one. So the fairy gives him nothing at all, and goes away. The lying woodcutter doesn't even get his old axe back, so he probably lost his job and starved. I liked reading the story, and the moral would be good for Ashley, but no way am I answering the review questions for her! No matter how hard she begs. And no matter what promises she makes.

*Facing page:*
**"The Honest Woodcutter"**

*Lynn Herr*
*Pencil on paper*
*Ashley's house*

*Lynn's comment:*
*This is from Ashley's reading assignment. I*
*also read it. There wasn't actually a duck in*
*the story, but I added one, so the pond would*
*look more like a pond. It still kind of just*
*looks like a big hole, though. And the duck*
*is floating over it, somehow. Oh well.*

There are a lot of regular books here, too. I mean books from stores, by authors. Books from schools always have questions after the stories. Real books don't, but they cost money. Maybe people are paying for not having to do the questions. This book I'm looking at now is full of drawings of the muscles and tendons Mrs Weir talks about when we do our exercises. I guess she memorized all the scientific names of things. But how did the artist know what all that stuff under the skin looks like? I hope it was just from looking at really muscular people.

I was trying to think of a new idea about what Aunt Celly's been doing and why I'm not allowed to go home. I already asked Mrs Weir for a hint, but that got me nowhere. She probably does know what's going on, though, since they're close friends. So it's probably something embarrassing or private, like a medical procedure. Oh, Aunt Celly isn't sick, is she? Is she having an operation? I really hope not! So Mrs Weir did finally give me a hint, about it not being anything like that, so I shouldn't worry. Well, that's a relief! But this whole thing is starting to bug me, for real.

Then Ashley said she knows the answer. Normally, when she knows a secret, she wants me to guess what it is. I never can, though. How am I supposed to guess a thing I'm not supposed to know about?

What Ashley just told me is the strangest thing I ever heard in my life.

I told Mrs Weir about it. She looked like she just saw a ghost. Then things went completely nuts here. The house practically turned upside-down, until Mrs Weir finally cornered Ashley.

This is really something. It's like they forgot I'm here. Ashley's mom didn't call it "an Important Question," so it wasn't official, but I know one when I hear it. A second and a third one, also. Because now Ashley's telling everything. Every single thing she did and heard. I can barely tell what she's saying through all the crying, though. This isn't like a regular scolding she tends to get. I've seen enough of those, before. Whatever this is, I'm not sure what to call it, but she's got to be in the biggest trouble of her life. Not really for spying on her mom and Aunt Celly, though. That was how she learned the secret. It's really because this was supposed to be Aunt Celly's decision, not anyone else's... not even Mrs Weir's, and certainly not Ashley's... about when, or whether or not at all, I should find out. But Ashley ruined it.

So now I know. I have a mom of my own. She's somewhere in town, this week. Aunt Celly is meeting with her. Maybe even right now. And I wasn't supposed to know anything about it, yet. Or maybe ever. But I thought Aunt Celly tells me everything. Even stuff she's not supposed to.

It's sort of unbelievable, but I guess it's really true. Of course, I've always had a mom. I would have to. That's how it works. But I don't know her. At all. I don't even know what her name is, or what she looks like. Or why I don't know her.

Mrs Weir is keeping me company. She asks how I'm feeling, not what I'm thinking. I feel really weird. It's like my head is moving around but it's actually not, or it's like half of me is trying to go somewhere but the other half isn't. Mrs Weir says that's perfectly normal and understandable. But she won't tell me any more than what I already found out from Ashley, because only Aunt Celly may do that. We have to wait for her to get back.

The worst thing is, I'm almost afraid to see her. Mrs Weir is also a little worried about it, since she'll have to break the news to Aunt Celly about the secret getting out. But no one is dreading it as much as Ashley.

*Facing page:*
**"Ashley Dreading It"**

*Lynn Herr*
*Pencil on paper*
*Ashley's house*

*Lynn's comment:*
*Ashley's bedroom door is the kind with*
*beads hanging down, instead of a big piece*
*of wood. It's so she can't slam or lock it,*
*anymore.*

~~~

Aunt Celly looked so sad and tired. But I think, also happy. She said I'm her wonderful Li'l Lynn, and she loves me. She was trying to protect me from maybe getting my hopes up and being disappointed. Or worse. That's why she kept this whole thing a secret from me, and why she's dealing with this now on the long weekend, and why she's been hiding me here at the Weirs' house. Because what if my mom showed up at my house or at my school, and tried to take me somewhere, and Aunt Celly didn't know about it?

Then Aunt Celly finally told me the stuff I didn't used to know about, from years ago. Family secrets. Those are the worst kind. About why my mom doesn't deserve me, after what that woman did to our family, and never took responsibility for, and never even apologized for. I didn't know there really was such a thing as abandoning a baby. That's awful. So my mom just plain bailed out, but my dad got his act together and handled things like a champion. That was the difference between them. And even after my dad died, my mom still didn't come back. That's why Aunt Celly has been taking care of me, for as long as I can remember. I think I understand why she never told me some parts of this, until now, and why she's been upset for such a long time. It's okay, really.

So back when I was just born, my mom wasn't ready to be a part of my life. But now, she thinks she is, at least in some way. She's been trying to prove that, to Aunt Celly. My mom wants to start getting to know me. I've been thinking about it, and I decided I want to meet her, too. We can, only if Aunt Celly lets us.

Right now, though, Aunt Celly says she has plans for Ashley. I wonder what that means.

*Facing page:*
*"The Biggest Day Ever"*

*Lynn Herr*
*Pencil on paper*
*At home*

*Lynn's comment:*
*I only met her once so far, but I remember*
*exactly what she looks like.  It was an*
*amazing day!*

# Denouement:

# Winter

Maybe Aunt Celly will never stop hating my mom, and never think she's any good. But I like knowing a little about my mom, better than not even knowing I have one. Someday, I'll have another visit with her, once she works through some more stuff. Maybe I'll even get to visit her where she lives. But that will be up to Aunt Celly, because she's still my legal guardian and isn't about to let that change. She did finally start depositing the checks my mom's been sending, though. It helps us out a lot.

Aunt Celly talks more about my dad than she used to. Funny stories. Things he liked to do, or wanted to do. What he liked more than anything else, in his last few years, was being my dad. I'm not sure if I actually remember him, at all. So I told Aunt Celly my earliest memories. The one about Colossus's wrinkles didn't give her much to go on. I also told Aunt Celly the one about seeing a frog in the backyard, and someone letting me know it was also there, the night before, but I couldn't remember who it was who told me.

She says it sure wasn't her.

## END

# Discussion Questions

*These may contain **SPOILERS** for the story.*

1.    In the early parts of the story, Lynn is contentedly close to Aunt Celly and Colossus, but makes no mention of having any friends, such as amongst her classmates. Do you think she is lonely, without realizing it? Does she "not know what she's missing," or does she wish to have like-minded friends, or is she just naturally a loner?

2.    As an extension of the previous question: Lynn initially views Ashley's attention as intrusive and irritating. Do you think this says more about Ashley's behavior, or about Lynn's disposition? In other words, is it more the case that Lynn is closed-minded, or that Ashley is unable to take a hint?

3.    Aunt Celly is in the habit of telling iffy stories to little Lynn. Why do you think she does this? Is it more to amuse herself, or from lack of satisfying peer relationships which would be conducive for such things, or is she actually trying to teach lessons to her young niece?

4.    In her narration to the reader, Lynn describes her own method of eating pizza and explains its benefits. Why, then, does she end up conforming to the Weirs' method, which she

believes is conducive to wastefulness?  Is she being considerate of her hosts, or is she fearful of their judgement, or is she actually not very confident about her preferred method?

5.      What do you think inspired Lynn to ask Aunt Celly about the phrase "I love you"?  What do you think was Lynn's actual question about it?  Do you agree that it is possible to overuse, misuse, or abuse emotionally potent pieces of language, to the point of exhausting or ruining them?  Or is it more the case that Aunt Celly is an emotionally distant person who has trouble connecting with others?

6.      Aunt Celly had been keeping her correspondence and meetings with Lynn's birthmother a secret from Lynn.  Do you think Aunt Celly's actual purpose in doing so was more to protect herself from being replaced, or to protect Lynn from a potentially toxic situation, or to spite the mother?  Was this justified?

7.      How Aunt Celly and Ashley will or will not get along with each other, following the chaotic incident during the long weekend, is not disclosed herein.  Do you expect this shake-up to be a permanent rift in their already strained relationship, or a bonding experience that will help them accept each other's relevance?

# *Would you*

*play along and*

# *write a letter to Li'l Lynn?*

Little Lynn "Li'l Lynn" Herr has expressed quite a few opinions within this tome of hers.  If you've got a word you'd like to have with her about something in particular, then why not send her a letter?  ...c/o her legal guardian, Celesta "Aunt Celly" Herr, of course.

Send your thoughtful message to

**auntcelly@charlesshearer.info**

and it might someday appear on

**https://charlesshearer.info**

# Scenario:
# "Coffee Shop"

*Originally appearing on the website for the graphic novel*
**Li'l Lynn: The Joy of Childhood and Other Myths**,
*the writing of this short piece pre-dated
the start of the novella-zation's production by about a year,
and served as the first experiment for exploring the characters
through prose instead of pictures and dialog.*

~~~

What better way to suss out the finicky and the high-maintenance from we regular folk, than to observe the behavior of potential culprits as they patronize a coffee shop? Our scenario, narrated soothingly with text alone, lest we become over-excited by the visual stimulus inherent in such riveting activity as is about to play out, is thus:

*Little Ashley and Lynn, together with their Mother Sandy and Aunt Celly, respectively, find themselves near a coffee shop.*

*Noticing this...*

...Ashley invites everyone inside.
...Lynn is reluctant to follow, having never been here before.
...Sandy offers to treat everyone.
...Celly cooperates, for the sake of indulging in luxury without having to spend her own money.

*Being a moderately popular suburban locale that is typically patronized by wealthy college students and staffed by poor college students, several customers are in line ahead of our heroes.*

*Having some time to kill...*

...Ashley wanders around, casing the joint.
...Lynn furtively glances around at the weirdos.
...Sandy thoughtfully studies the menu, as if having never seen it before.
...Celly, upon careful inspection of the staff, is relieved to not recognize anyone from when she used to work here.

*The coffee shop's menu is a complicated array of exotic names, relative sizes, and fixed numerals that are organized into an artfully disguised chart, with season-appropriate graphical decorations and an appetite-inducing color scheme.*

*Confronted with such a spectacle and coerced into making an immediate decision...*

...Ashley returns from her exploration and decisively places her order first.
...Lynn, unequipped for the abundance of incomprehensible options, wisely delegates the task to a specialist.
...Ashley changes her first order to something else.
...Sandy places the same complicated order that she always does.
...Celly, suddenly recalling traumatic memories of high-maintenance customers, orders the simplest possible item.
...Ashley is sure, this time: her first order was the right one.

*The current employees on duty, being only human and therefore fallible, as well as new to the job and chronically sleep-deprived, are neither exceedingly accurate with details nor expertly proficient with the various pieces of noisy equipment.*

*Waiting for the orders to be ready...*

...Ashley stays by the pick-up counter, watching the staff, suggesting improvements to them.

...Lynn, unsure of what was ordered on her behalf, asks for an explanation.

...Sandy picks out a place for everyone to sit, waiting for the orders' completion to be announced.

...Celly stays close to the counter but faces away from it, hating how some customers used to critique her work.

*Once the orders are served, our heroes take their seats and leisure time commences in earnest, with conversation, the consumption of respective beverages, and other reasonable activities.*

*Sampling their drinks...*

...Ashley doubts that hers is right, but her mother, conducting a taste test, verifies its accuracy.

...Lynn, having no idea whether hers is right or not, can not decide if she likes it.

...Sandy detects a considerable error with hers, politely swapping it for a correct one.

...Celly, who had low expectations and ordered what was the least likely to go wrong, is perfectly satisfied with what she thinks is the "house blend."

*As the encounter continues...*

...Ashley is even more sure, this time: her other order would have been the right one.

...Lynn pretends that she is actually drinking hers.

...Sandy manages to enjoy half of hers, the other half being donated to a worthy cause, i.e. consoling Ashley.

...Celly, who sees right through Lynn's act and mercifully relieves her of duty, ends up drinking nearly two whole cups.

*Before a great while more has passed, the day is done and the party disbands. Under the cloud-speckled evening sky, Ashley returns home with her mother, and Lynn and her Aunt Celly return to their own abode.*

*This episode shall pass into legend! but in the meanwhile...*

...Ashley, inspired by the interesting machinery that she had witnessed, teaches herself how to use the coffee maker in the kitchen.
...Lynn is satisfyingly exhausted from such a fun excursion, and soon falls asleep.
...Sandy, hating to let anything go to waste, puts the coffee in the freezer, for tomorrow.
...Celly spends most of the night wide awake, envying her niece.

~~~

## REVIEW QUESTIONS:

1.     Why do you think Celly was relieved to not recognize any of the staff members?

2.     Why do you think the staff pretended not to recognize Celly?

3.     What do you think the staff actually meant by telling Ashley that she is "so helpful right now"?


4.     What do you think is the best way for the staff to passive-aggressively avenge themselves upon customers who, for the sake of making room in their cups by some method other than drinking all of for what they had paid, pour some of their coffee into the easily punctured trash bags which the staff will later have to lift out of the receptacle and lug all the way to the dumpster that is located behind one of the shops that is several buildings away?

A Vertical Bonus Comic
Made Exclusively for Inclusion in

# LI'L LYNN
## Tells It Herself

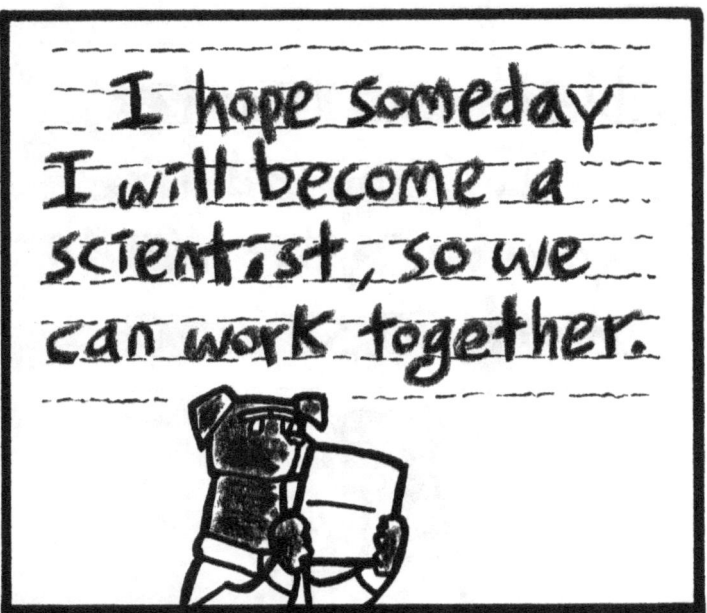

## Finished and Avowed Works by Charles Shearer

Graphic Novels
  *Li'l Lynn: The Joy of Childhood and Other Myths*
  *Runaway Weer the Burdened*
  *Runaway Weer the Corrupted*
  *Runaway Weer the Accused*
  *The Runaway Weer Addenda*

Illustrated Prose
  *The Answer Lies in Oz*
  *Upon the Name of Oz*
  *Li'l Lynn Tells It Herself: A Novella-zation*
  *Sootwork-Mauzi*
  *Brevitous Accounts of Fictional Incidents*

**https://charlesshearer.info**

# THE ARCANE·APOCRYPHA

*makes ready to receive you...*